little
EXCAVATOR

FUTURE PARK SITE

little EXCAVATOR

Anna Dewdney

VIKING

Here come the BIG RIGS,
rolling down the street.

Thumpa-thumpa bumpa-bumpa

BEEP BEEP BEEP!

Can you see **LITTLE E**, ready on the spot?

He's the **LITTLE EXCAVATOR** working on the lot.

Whammm! goes the 'DOZER, knocking down the walls.

Rumble-rumble crumble-crumble

FALL
FALL
FALL!

Little E is busy—
he goes

Uh-oh, Little Excavator. . . .
Now you're in a jam.

GrrrrrrRrarrrrrrm! goes the LOADER,
lifting up the trash!

Pusha-pusha smusha-smusha SMASH

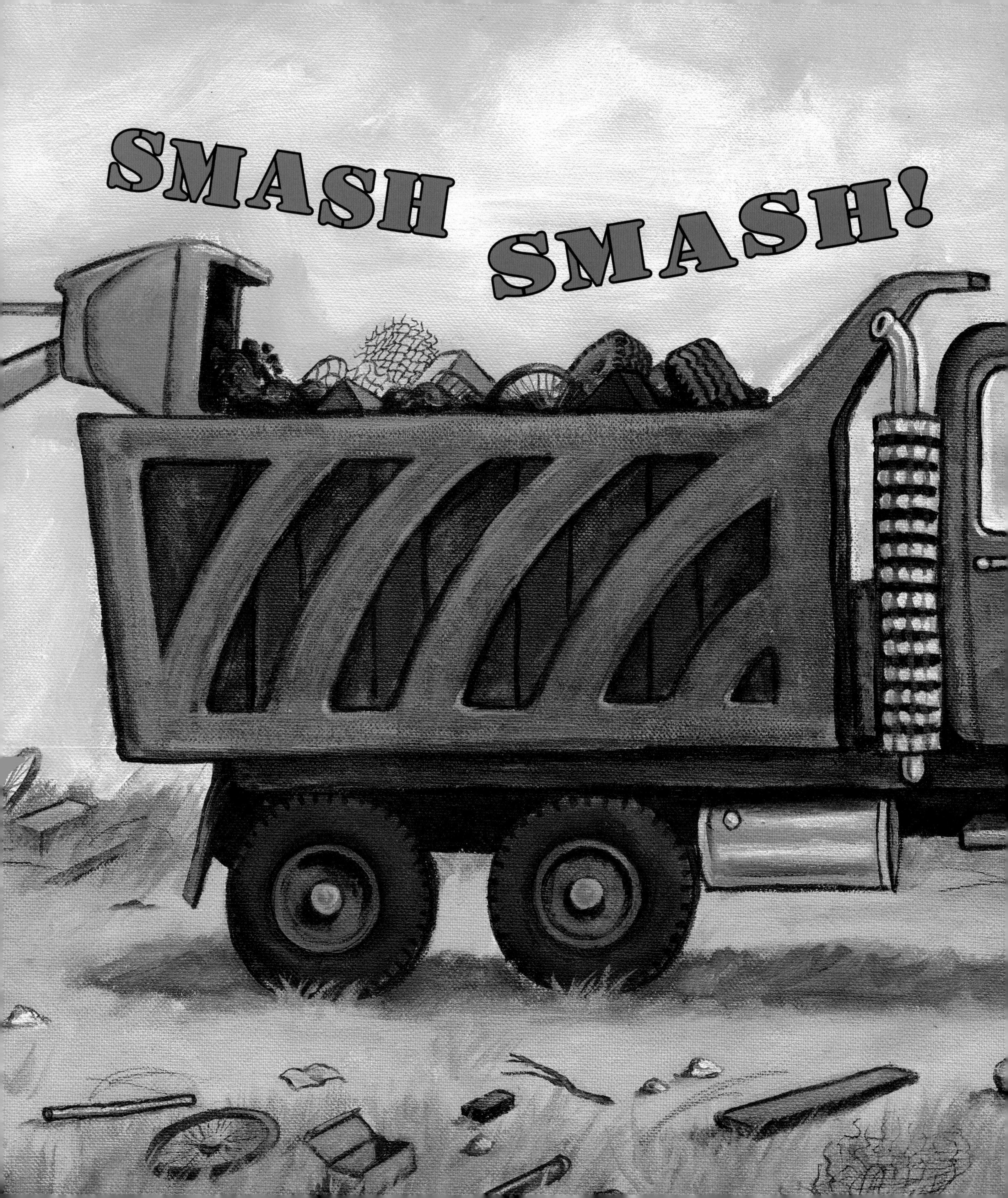
SMASH
SMASH!

Little E tries lifting up some

junk

junk

junk!

But there goes Little Excavator—
over with a clunk!

Drrroooom! goes the DUMP TRUCK,
with a load to lug.

Thunka-thunka clunka-clunka

CHUG CHUG
CHUG!

Little E just wants to lug all

day day day!

Look out, Little Excavator—
don't get in the way!

Brrrrump! goes the BACKHOE,
digging in the dirt.

Clang-clang bang-bang

WORK WORK WORK!

Little E is helping, too—he can  dig

dig

 dig!

Not yet, Little Excavator. . . .
Someday when you're big.

Whirrrrrr! goes the tall CRANE,
rising to the sky.

Whoosh-whoosh swoosh-swoosh HIGH

HIGH

Little E is stretching— he gets **tall**

tall

tall!

Sorry, Little Excavator—
you're too small.

Now there's **one last job**
and the busy day is done.

But no BIG RIG can do it. . . .
Not a **single one**.

Everybody tries it

and it's

much

too

tight....

But can it be? Little E . . .

fits just right!

Good job, Little Excavator!

Time to take a bow.

There's work to do, just for you, HERE and NOW.

You may be small, Little E,
but you will grow. . . .

You're a **MIGHTY LITTLE EXCAVATOR . . .**

GO GO GO!

*For little diggers
everywhere.*

VIKING
Penguin Young Readers Group
An imprint of Penguin Random House LLC
Visit us at penguinrandomhouse.com

First published in the United States of America by Viking,
an imprint of Penguin Random House LLC, 2017

LIBRARY OF CONGRESS CATALOGING-IN-PUBLICATION DATA IS AVAILABLE
ISBN: 9781101999202
Special Markets ISBN 9780451480422 Not for Resale

Printed in China   Set in GeoSlab730

5   7   9   10   8   6   4